KINGS OF THE CASTLE

For Lucy

A TEMPLAR BOOK

First published in the UK in 2016 by Templar Publishing,
part of the Bonnier Publishing Group,
The Plaza, 535 King's Road, London, SW10 0SZ
www.templarco.co.uk
www.bonnierpublishing.com

Copyright © 2016 by Victoria Turnbull

1 3 5 7 9 10 8 6 4 2

ISBN 978-1-78370-258-9 (Hardback)
ISBN 978-1-78370-259-6 (Paperback)

Designed by Verity Clark
Edited by Katie Haworth

Printed in China

KINGS OF THE CASTLE

Victoria Turnbull

t

templar publishing

George didn't want to waste
the night moonbathing.

He wanted to
build a sandcastle

that would turn
any monster

green eyed
with envy . . .

. . . but Boris had other ideas.

When out of the sea . . .

What on Earth?

. . . came the strangest looking
creature George had ever seen.

George decided to introduce himself – the creature couldn't be worse company than Boris.

But it was hopeless.

They could not understand

one another.

. . . but Boris had other ideas.

Maybe they could be friends after all.

And so with a
little planning . . .

. . . George and Nepo set to work.

And before long, the flag
could be raised.

George and Nepo
had done it.
They were now . . .

They reigned until dawn.

When the tide came in and the sun came up,

they headed for home.

The night was over . . .

. . . but some things last forever.

Also by Victoria Turnbull

THE
SEA
TIGER

"I am the sea tiger.
I am Oscar's best friend.
Together, we travel to
EXTRAORDINARY PLACES
under a sea studded
with stars."

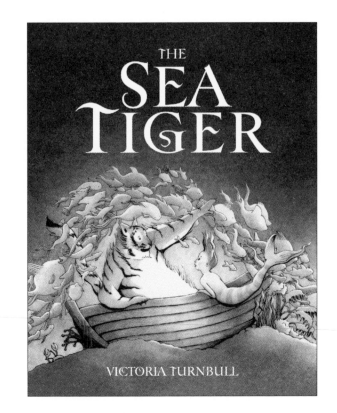

RRP £12.99 – ISBN 978-1-78370-006-6 (HB)
RRP £7.99 – ISBN 978-1-78370-007-3 (PB)

'. . . lyrical, elegiac and highly imaginative' – winner of
the 2013 Association of Illustrators New Talent Award,
Children's Book category

Victoria Turnbull was born in York, and spent her childhood absorbed by books and drawing.

After studying Graphic Design at Staffordshire University, she went on to take up a place on the MA in Children's Book Illustration at the Cambridge School of Art, graduating in 2013.

As part of her MA, Victoria created a picture book, *The Sea Tiger,* which has seen her named the winner of the Association of Illustrators New Talent Award 2013 (Children's Book Category) and was published by Templar in June 2014. *The Sea Tiger* was also shortlisted for the Waterstones Children's Book Prize, 2015.

Victoria now lives in London, where she both writes and illustrates her own stories.